For Baby Anna. Welcome to my ever-expanding funny family.

Thanks to Lauren for your help and enthusiasm.

Chris Higgins
Illustrated by Lee Wildish

HODDER CHILDREN'S BOOKS

First published in Great Britain in 2016 by Hodder and Stoughton

1 3 5 7 9 10 8 6 4 2

Text copyright © Chris Higgins 2016
Illustrations © Lee Wildish 2016

A CIP catalogue record for this book is available from the British Library.

ISBN 978-1-444-92577-7

Typeset in SabonInfant by Avon DataSet Ltd, Bidford on Avon, Warwickshire
Printed and bound in Great Britain by Clays Ltd, St Ives plc

The paper and board used in this book are made from wood from responsible sources.

MIX
Paper from
responsible sources
FSC® C104740
www.fsc.org

Chapter 1

My name is Mattie and I'm a worrier.

I worry about everything.

Big things, little things.

Silly things, sad things.

Things that have happened, things that are going to happen, things that may never happen.

I can't help it, I was born this way. And I don't just worry about me: I worry for my whole family.

Somebody has to.

Today I am more worried than I have ever been in my whole life. I am beside myself with worry.

Except, to be strictly honest, I can't actually *be* beside myself because I can't move.

I'm strapped into my seat and I can't get out. None of us can.

It's quiet.

Not peaceful quiet.

Deadly quiet.

No one else seems to realise the danger we're in.

Out of the silence comes a faint rumble. Grandma, who is sitting next to me, looks up. The rumble grows into a grumble and changes to a growl.

'Grandma!' I whisper urgently but she can't hear me because the noise is getting louder by the second. It's like an angry lion, prowling around us, ready to pounce. The hairs on the back of my neck stand on end.

Suddenly there's a jolt and I lurch forward. It's got me!

I tug at my belt, struggling to free myself. 'I want to get out!'

Grandma pats my hand. Dontie stares out of the window ignoring me, as if I'm embarrassing him.

What is wrong with them? Nobody cares that we're trapped, except me. This is a nightmare!

We jerk forward again and I shriek.

'Calm down, Mattie,' says Mum's soothing voice from in front of me. I can't see her but I know she's there. 'There's nothing to be afraid of.'

She's wrong. We're moving faster now, building up speed.

'*Mum!* I want to sit by you!'

But she can't hear me. I couldn't get up if I tried. The noise is deafening now, blasting me back into my seat. It vibrates around me, no, *through* me, like a manic ghost, whooshing and rattling, shuddering and juddering!

I grab hold of Dontie's and Grandma's hands, hold tight, and close my eyes.

My ears are about to explode. My head is about to burst.

I should've made a Worry List.

And then ... I feel myself soaring ... up, up, up into the air ...

The noise fades ...

It's over.

Cautiously, I open my eyes. Through

the window the sky is a brilliant blue
I've never seen before and there are fluffy
white clouds that look as if I could stand
on them.

Is this heaven?

I clap my hands and cheer.

'Hurray! We're flying!'

Chapter 2

We're going to Australia! The whole of
the Butterfield family, including Grandma
and Granddad and Uncle Vesuvius. It's a
long way away, on the other side of the
world.

It will take us a whole day and night to
get there!

Uncle Bruce and Aunty Sheila live
there. They paid for our tickets. All of us!
They're soooooo kind.

I've never flown before, but I expect

you've worked that out already. It was really scary taking off but now we're up in the air, it's fun.

We've flown over so many different countries we've lost count. It's OK though, Dad says he's keeping track, to make sure the pilot doesn't go the wrong way.

He's sitting in the row in front of me (Dad, I mean, not the pilot). So is Mum, baby Will, Stanika and V.

In case you've forgotten, Stanika is two people, Stanley (who's five) and Anika (three). They're always together so it's easier to call them Stanika. V is eight.

There are so many of us we spread over the aisles.

I'm sitting in the row behind with Dontie who's twelve and Grandma,

Granddad and Uncle Vesuvius who are old. I'm Mattie and I'm nine. And, like I said, I'm a bit of a worrier.

I'm not worried anymore though. I'm eating my lunch. Only it's dinner, because we are flying over different time zones and we've got to catch up with Australia where it's tomorrow already!

I am learning so much and I'm not even there yet.

Dinner is delicious. The air stewardess brings me a special meal so that I and the other vegetarians on the plane don't have to choose between chicken or beef, and it comes before everyone else's.

It's on a tray, like school dinners, only there's more of it and it's got a serviette.

'I wish I was vegetarian,' moans Dontie, watching me tuck into my melon

starter followed by lentil and bean bake. 'I'm starving!'

It's delicious. There's lemon mousse for afters, and cheese and biscuits, and just when I think I'm completely stuffed I find a chocolate in a shiny wrapper in my cup.

And we can have whatever drinks we like. Dontie and I order coke before Mum notices.

'Glass of red please,' says Granddad.

'Just an orange juice,' says Grandma. 'Too early in the day for me.'

'It's the middle of the night in Australia,' says Uncle Vesuvius cheerfully and he orders a glass of red too. 'I'm on holiday.'

'To Australia!' says Granddad, holding up his glass, and we all clink each other's glasses and say, 'Cheers!'

I'm glad I'm sitting in this row and not the one in front. Anika's crying because she's tipped her juice and V is complaining because it's tipped over her. Mum's trying to mop it up but she's feeding baby Will and there's not much room.

But it's OK. The nice stewardess comes along to sort it out. Everyone settles down and before long, baby Will and Stanika drift off to sleep.

Uncle Vez and Granddad drift off to sleep too. You can hear them snoring. I breathe a big sigh of happiness as I gaze out at the beautiful blue sky and sip my drink. I feel really grown up.

'Want to watch a movie?' asks Dontie and he folds my table away so I can watch it on my very own screen which is on the back of Mum's chair. I've got my own earphones too so Dontie and I don't even have to watch the same one.

I LOVE flying.

Chapter 3

When most people think of Australia they think of Sydney Harbour Bridge and Sydney Opera House. Sydney is on the east coast.

We are flying into Perth on the west coast.

Australia is a huge country. Did you know that crossing from Sydney to Perth is like travelling from Moscow to London? That's how big it is!

Aunty Sheila told us. She lives on a

farm in Western Australia, or WA as she calls it, with Uncle Bruce who's Uncle Vez's brother.

They came to visit us and we were really sad when they had to leave. But now we are going to see them again!

We have to change planes sometime in the middle of the night somewhere in the middle of the world but I miss landing because I'm asleep. On the next plane I go straight back to sleep and don't wake up until we're nearly in Australia.

This time I notice that coming down is easier than going up. We have to put our seats in the upright position and fasten our safety belts and suddenly, with a bump and a bounce, we've landed. The plane feels like it's going really fast when we hit the ground but soon it slows down and comes to a stop.

'We're here!' shouts Stanley and everyone on the plane cheers. It's taken a long time.

'I can't wait to see Uncle Bruce and Aunty Sheila,' says V. Me too.

When you get off the plane you have to show your passports or they won't let you into the country. We've all got one, even baby Will. Anika had to have her photo taken five times because she kept laughing and you're not allowed to laugh in a passport photo. You're not even allowed to smile.

I show mine to the passport officer. He looks at me sternly and my heart starts banging.

Worry Alert! I must've smiled by mistake. He's not going to let me in.

But it's OK. He hands my passport back and says, 'Welcome to Australia, Matisse. That's a pretty name.'

'It's Mattie for short,' I explain. 'Like Uncle Vesuvius. That's him, standing behind me. We call him Uncle Vez but his real name is Albert Trot.'

The passport officer holds out his hand for Uncle Vez's passport and studies him with a frown. I worry that I shouldn't have said that his real name is Albert Trot but it's OK, it's in his passport, so he is allowed in too.

Everyone else gets in as well, even Will who's got a really stinky nappy.

I think passport officers are supposed to look stern but they're nice really.

We wait for our luggage in a big hall with all the other people from our plane.

It arrives on a moving belt that goes round and round in a circle and Dad and Granddad and Dontie have to grab our bags before they sail past.

'Nine, ten, eleven,' says Dad, counting. 'That's it, they're all here. That was surprisingly easy. All ready to go!'

What a relief. I was worried when we'd changed planes in the middle of the night. I wanted to get my backpack out of the hold and carry it onto the next plane myself but Dad explained that wasn't the way it works. They have special baggage handlers who do that for you so they don't get lost.

'Where's Will's buggy?' asks Mum.

Ping! Ping! **Worry Alert**. I knew this would happen!

A man from the airport goes off to see

if he can find it. He's gone for ages.

Some other people have been waiting for ages for their luggage too. They look fed up.

Will is very wriggly because Mum and Dad have held him all the way from England to Australia so Dad puts him down on the luggage belt.

When the fed up people see baby Will sailing past them between a case and a surfboard, they cheer up and say, 'Aahh!'

Anika wants a ride too so when Will comes around again Dad puts her and

Stanley on the carousel next to him. The cheered-up people wave at them all as they go round and round.

'Can I have a go?' asks V.

'Let's all have a go!' says Uncle Vez and pretends to climb on and the cheered-up people laugh and clap. But the airport man comes back at that moment with Will's buggy and tells Uncle Vez off.

'Right!' says Mum, stuffing Will into the buggy. 'Pick your bag up, everyone! Let's get out of here before they send us back to where we came from for causing a public nuisance!'

'Quick!' I say, spotting the 'exit' sign. 'Follow me.'

I lead the way into the Arrivals Hall and stop in surprise. A huge crowd of people are waiting to greet us with signs and flowers and helium balloons saying *Welcome to Australia.*

I feel like a celebrity!

Then I notice that the signs people are holding up all have different names on them but none of them says, *The Butterfields.*

Worry Alert!

Chapter 4

'Where are Norman and Audrey?' asks Uncle Vez, peering around. Norman and Audrey are Uncle Bruce and Aunty Sheila's real names. We go in for nicknames in our family.

'No sign of them,' says Granddad.

'Have they forgotten we're coming?' asks V, crossly, and my heart sinks.

All of a sudden I spot something at the back of the crowd. 'Look!'

Balloons on long strings! One, two

three, four, five, six, seven, eight, nine, ten, eleven of them, each one with a drawn-on smiley face and a hat with corks on which bob about as they sway to and fro.

'It's us!' I shout. 'The Butterfields!'

'It's them!' V shouts. 'Uncle Bruce and Aunty Sheila!'

And we race each other through the crowds into Uncle Bruce and Aunty Sheila's wide-open arms.

Outside the airport we pile into a bright yellow mini-bus that Uncle Bruce has hired to fit us all in. Most of our luggage has to go on top. I'm sooooo excited.

'First one to see a kangaroo gets a nice, shiny Australian dollar!' says Aunty Sheila, as we all squash inside with our balloon family.

'There's one!' shouts Anika, but she's fibbing.

I don't care about the dollar. I just want to see a kangaroo.

Dontie gets to ride in the front next to Uncle Bruce.

'That's not fair!' says V automatically as she climbs into the back. Then Anika's balloon pops and she cries so Stanley gives her his.

We trail our balloon family out of the window but one by one they pop and the hats blow off. Dontie has to keep jumping out to rescue them. Only Grandma and Granddad's balloons survive.

'Never mind,' says Aunty Sheila. 'So long as you've got the hats. You'll need them where you're going.'

When we leave the airport and pull out into the traffic to take our first look at Australia, I'm a bit puzzled.

'That's funny, Aunty Sheila, I thought you said there were lots of kangaroos.'

'And koalas,' says V, her nose pressed flat against the window.

'And kookaburras,' says Anika, who's been clutching her toy one all the way from England.

'And crocodiles,' says Stanley, sounding a bit flat.

All we can see are high office buildings, shops, houses, roads and lots of traffic.

'Where's the ocean?' asks Dontie, who's dying to learn to surf.

'Over there,' says Uncle Bruce, nodding his head to the right.

We turn to look but it's nowhere to be seen.

'I thought there would be blue skies,' says Mum, inspecting the grey clouds.

'I thought it would be sunny,' says Grandma, staring gloomily at the rain.

'I thought it would be different,' says Stanley, sadly, 'but it's the same.'

'Just like home,' says V, disappointed.

'Aw, stop whinging you lot,' says Aunty Sheila cheerfully, as Uncle Bruce weaves his way through the traffic. 'We'll be out of the city in a sec. Then you'll see the real Australia.'

Before long we come to a crossroads and Uncle Bruce turns left, away from the ocean. The road is bumpier now. First the office buildings disappear, then the shops. Soon all there is to see is just the odd house at the side of the road with a tin roof and a tin fence.

This is more like it.

I still haven't seen a kangaroo though.

Chapter 5

After a while we stop at a roadhouse to fill up with petrol. A roadhouse is like a motorway service station only smaller and without the motorway. Uncle Bruce buys us fish and chips and I cheer up, even though I just have cheesy chips because I'm vegetarian.

'Is it a long way to your farm?' asks V.

'Everywhere's a long way in Australia,' says Uncle Bruce, and then we're on the road again.

Full up with food, everyone nods off one by one, until only Uncle Bruce and I are still awake. Uncle Bruce is driving and I'm watching out for kangaroos.

After a while we turn again and now the road is just one long straight strip of red earth disappearing into the distance. Clouds of red dust rise into the air as we bowl along.

In the front, Uncle Bruce is singing a song to himself about gum trees and sheep and kangaroos and verandas and old rocking chairs.

I can see gum trees out of the window, real ones, standing tall and straight. I can see sheep too. At last Australia is beginning to feel real.

Suddenly I sit bolt upright. I've spotted something.

'Uncle Bruce! What's that?'

'What's what?'

'Over there! Look!'

He peers through his mirror. 'It's a paddock, Mattie.'

'What's a paddock?' I've never heard of this creature.

Uncle Bruce yawns. 'That's what we call a field in Australia.'

'No! I saw something else! Something *in* the paddock!'

'It'll be sheep. This country's full of them.'

'It didn't look like a sheep,' I say, but he's stopped listening.

Sheep don't normally sit up on their back legs and hop gracefully across the grass, do they? Well, they don't at home, but maybe they do in Australia?

We are whizzing along now and I keep looking, but we're going too fast and the light is starting to fade. I'm feeling a bit down. It's nearly the end of my first day in Australia and I haven't seen a kangaroo.

Maybe I'll never get to see one.

All of a sudden there's a long, loud blast of noise and everyone wakes up.

'What on earth is that?' asks Dad.

'Road train,' says Uncle Bruce and he pulls into the side of the road to let a huge truck hurtle past. It's the biggest one I've ever seen in my life and it's pulling six carriages!

'Awesome!' breathes Dontie.

'Oh, wow!' I exclaim.

'I didn't know you were into trucks, Mattie love,' says Aunty Sheila, giving me a squashy hug.

'No, look!' I point at the window.

Bounding away from the road, in flight from the road train monster, is a family of kangaroos.

Chapter 6

After that we see more and more of them. Big ones, little ones and baby ones. Some kangaroos hop away when they see our bright yellow mini-bus coming, but others are brave and stare at us.

'We're not as scary as the road train,' says Mum.

It's so exciting. We keep spotting them and shouting to each other.

V: 'Look at him standing by his mum and dad! He's so cute!'

Me: 'I like that one peeping out of its mum's pouch. You can only see its head.'

V: 'It looks like Will in his buggy.'

Stanley: 'Will, you're a kangaroo!'

Will: 'Chuckle, chuckle, hiccup.'

Aunty Sheila: 'The mum's probably got a smaller one in her pouch as well.'

Dontie: 'She'll need a double-buggy!'

Aunty Sheila: 'Nah! They're just tiddlers when they're born. They only measure an inch or two.'

Me: 'Honest?'

Aunty Sheila: 'Aw yeah. They stay in their mum's pouch feeding non-stop till they're big enough to fend for themselves.'

Mum: 'Sounds familiar.'

Aunty Sheila: 'Basically as soon as a fully-grown female kangaroo has given birth she gets pregnant again.'

Dad: 'Definitely sounds familiar.'

V: 'The baby ones are called joeys.'

Stanley: 'My friend is called Joey!'

V: 'Ha! Ha! Your friend's a kangaroo!'

Uncle Bruce slows down to a stop and sticks his head out of the window. A kangaroo is lying on the road, propped up on his elbow, soaking up the last of the evening sun.

'Excuse me, mate,' says Uncle Bruce politely. 'D'you mind moving over?'

The kangaroo stares at Uncle Bruce as if to say, 'Who's going to make me?' and stays right where he is.

'Young boomer,' says Uncle Bruce. 'Thinks he owns the place.'

The kangaroo turns his gaze on me. He's got a distinctive white E-shape on his chest and his eyes are soft and brown with long, dark lashes. He's very handsome.

I smile at him. He lumbers to his feet, bounces to the side of the road, stops and looks back, as if to say, 'Is that OK?'

'Perfect,' says Uncle Bruce, raising his hat to him. 'Much obliged. Now stay off the blooming road!'

The kangaroo winks at me.

I keep looking back at him as we drive on. He's still standing there in the semi-darkness, watching us. I give him a wave and he waves back.

He's my friend. I'm going to call him ... Eric.

'Boomer like that could cause a nasty

accident if we drove into him in the dark,' remarks Uncle Bruce.

'You'd think they'd have the sense to keep off the road, wouldn't you?' says Granddad.

'They do, during the day. But when the sun goes down, the road stays warm, so the daft critters come and lie down on it to go to sleep.'

Oh no! Poor Eric. I hope he doesn't get run over.

And then something strange happens.

Normally I'd worry about this all night long. But I know that Eric will stay off the road now Uncle Bruce has told him to.

He's not a daft critter at all.

He understood.

Chapter 7

It's pitch dark when we get to Uncle Bruce and Aunty Sheila's farm. The moon is high in the black velvety sky and billions of stars are winking down at us.

As we get out of the bus we stand and stare up at them.

'Sparkles!' says Anika, in delight.

'Magic!' breathes Stanley.

'I've never seen so many stars in my whole life,' cries Mum.

'They're in the wrong place!' shouts

Dontie. 'Where's the Great Bear? Where's the Plough?'

'On the other side of the world,' explains Uncle Bruce. 'We've got our own constellations, Down Under. Look! There's the Southern Cross.'

I can see it now he's pointed it out. A hazy white cross is hanging above us in the sky.

Dad puts his hand on my shoulder. 'There are billions of stars up there, Mattie!'

'Do you think there's someone up there looking down at us, Dad?' I whisper.

His eyes are shining. 'Who knows? On a night like tonight, anything is possible.'

The farmhouse door opens and three dogs come tearing out, barking a welcome with their tails wagging furiously.

'Jellico!' screams Anika, but it's not. Our dog has been left at home, well, at Rupert Rumble's house actually (Stan's friend). One of the dogs rushing towards us looks like him, pointy-nosed and scruffy. (Jellico, I mean, not Rupert Rumble.)

'It's Bandit!' I shout. I've heard all about these three.

Bandit's a collie cross, like Jellico, Bess is a full-bred collie and Bluey is a short-haired Blue Heeler, bred to be an Australian cattle dog, though they're used for rounding up sheep too. They tear around us in excited circles, leaping up at us and barking their heads off.

'Welcome to Australia!' calls a warm, throaty voice, just like Aunty Sheila's. I can see the outline of a figure against

the light in the doorway, big and round. It comes towards us with outstretched arms. More figures come spilling out behind her.

'It's Lorabelle!' booms Aunty Sheila. One by one Lorabelle gives us kids a hug and it's just like being hugged by Aunty Sheila, all soft and squashy. She smells like her too, warm and sugar-sweet.

'We've made you some damper, cos Mum said you liked it,' Lorabelle says and then I know what the smell is. Maple syrup. Yum. 'Thought you might be peckish after your journey.'

'We stopped for fish and chips,' explains Stanley.

'Good on you, mate!' says Lorabelle cheerfully. She's a younger version of Aunty Sheila, large and jolly and sounds like her too. 'Big guy like you could always make room for a bit of damper though?'

Stanley nods happily. The Butterfields can always make room for damper.

'We've got Milo too,' says a voice. It's a girl a few years older than me, with fair hair in a pony-tail, big eyes, and long legs in skimpy shorts.

'What's Milo?' I ask.

The girl shrugs. 'Milo!' she says as if that explains it. She's very pretty. A boy is standing next to her, about my age, one hand resting on Bluey's collar.

'Come on in and try it,' says Lorabelle, and she picks up Anika. 'This is Mitch, my old man.' She indicates a long, stringy man, nearly as tall as Mr McGibbon at my school who's the tallest man I know. '... And these guys are Summer and Jayden,' she continues.

The adults go into hand-shaking, head-nodding, back-slapping, good-to-meet-you mode while the kids study each other silently.

'Summer? That's not a name,' says V. 'It's a season.'

'Ha ha!' says Summer. I like her name.

It suits her because she's bright and sunny. 'What are you called?'

'V.'

'That's not a name, that's a letter,' says Jayden.'

He looks like his sister with big eyes, a thick fringe and the same wide, friendly grin.

I'm glad V said that, not me. I've already made myself look silly asking about Milo – and I *still* don't know what it is.

Australia is full of surprises.

'What about you guys?' asks Jayden.

'I'm Mattie.'

'I'm Stanley and she's Anika.'

'What's the baby called?'

'Will.'

'Ahhh!' Summer chucks him under the

chin and he laughs. Then she says to me, 'It's easy to see who Uncle Albert is.'

'Who?'

She points at Uncle Vesuvius. 'Uncle Albert. Granddad's brother. They're the spitting image of each other. Albert and Norman.'

'We don't call them that,' says V. 'We call them Uncle Vez and Uncle Bruce.'

'Why?'

V opens her mouth to explain but does a huge yawn instead which makes me start yawning too. Tiredness settles over my shoulders like a warm blanket.

Summer looks at us curiously, then turns her attention to Dontie.' What are you called?'

'Dontie.'

I blink in surprise at my cool brother.

He's gone pink. I've never seen him do that before in my life. Then he mumbles, 'Donatello, actually.'

'Donatello, *actually*!' Summer repeats with a cheeky grin, displaying perfect white teeth. 'Awesome!'

Dontie's pink cheeks deepen to bright red and he turns away. What is *wrong* with him?

Worry Alert!

These people must think we're seriously weird.

I bet they think my funny family is not just from the other side of the world.

I bet they think we're from another planet.

Chapter 8

I wake up and don't know where I am.

It's daylight.

Beside me, V is snoring peacefully.

Somewhere outside a cock is crowing and a dog is barking. Two dogs. No, three.

I'm on the farm.

I'm in Australia!

I pull my leg out from under V's, turn onto my back and make a mental list of things I can remember about last night.

1. the crowded kitchen

2. the noisy adults

3. sitting by the wood-stove

4. eating damper with maple syrup

5. drinking Milo (which turned out to be a hot, milky drink, a bit like Ovaltine)

6. leaning against Mum's legs. She was stroking my hair. It was warm and cosy and smelt of wood-smoke. I closed my eyes and let the buzz of adult voices and laughter melt over me like warm chocolate.

That was the last thing I could remember.

'Hi!'

A head appears from above, upside down, long, loose fair hair hanging down like a waterfall, arms dangling below it. For a moment I think it's Lily Pickles, V's best friend from home, who loves hanging upside-down.

But of course it's not because Lily Pickles is the other side of the world. It's Summer. She's on the top bunk, V and I are on the bottom.

I sit up and bang my head. *Ouch!*

'You snore, Mattie.'

'No I don't. V does.'

She listens. V is still asleep. 'Oh yeah.' Summer studies me, still upside down. 'What d'you want to do today?'

'Can I look round your farm?'

'OK. It's pretty big though.'

'Can I see your top paddock?'

'What for?'

'You've got kangaroos in it. Aunty Sheila showed me a photo.'

'Aunty Sheila? You mean Gran.' Summer studies me, her eyes close to mine only the wrong way up. 'You're funny.'

'You are!' I say.

'You are!' she copies me.

'You are!' I repeat and we both burst out laughing and wake V up.

In the kitchen Aunty Sheila is frying eggs and there's a queue for breakfast.

'Come on,' says Summer, 'I'll show you the top paddock while we're waiting.'

'Wait for me!' shouts Jayden.

We run outside. Immediately we're surrounded by flies. Buzzing crazily, they dive-bomb us, searching out our eyes, ears, noses, mouths.

'Aaghhhh!' shouts V, waving her arms wildly. 'Do they bite?'

'Only the big ones,' says Summer, but I think she's joking. 'Hats!' She hands us our hats with the bobbing corks which are on a line of hooks on the verandah.

We follow her and Jayden up through fields of sheep and ploughed earth which Summer explains is waiting to be planted with wheat. The sun is already hot even though it's very early morning and there are flies, flies, flies, everywhere! I'm glad I've got my hat on because it shades me from the sun *and* keeps the pesky critters away (that's what Jayden calls them).

Soon we come to water. It's a cross between a big pond and a small lake.

'This is our dam,' says Jayden proudly. Stanley and I did an Australian to English dictionary when Uncle Bruce and Aunty Sheila came to visit, so I knew what it was.

'Can we swim in it?' V hops around on one leg, trying to tug off her shoe. 'I'm a really good swimmer!'

I roll my eyes. She's such a show-off. Summer grins. 'If you want,' she says. 'Watch out for the crocs.'

V stops hopping about and her jaw drops open in alarm.

Summer bursts out laughing. 'Just kidding! You might get your toes nibbled by the yabbies, though.'

'What are yabbies?' asks V, suspiciously.

'I know! I know!' I shout. 'Uncle Bruce told us about them. They're big prawns, right?'

'Kind of,' says Summer. 'Those guys like to come and drink from it too.'

'Which guys?'

'Duh!' She points to a group of trees in the distance. I screw my eyes up and can just make out shapes huddled in the shade underneath.

Suddenly the penny drops. 'Oh, wow! Are those—'

'Kangaroos!' squeals V and makes a dash towards them.

'Watch out for the big boys!' shouts

Summer. 'They can be a bit unpredictable.'

A large kangaroo uncurls, gets to its feet and hops away from the shade of the trees. He stands up tall on his hind legs and V stops uncertainly.

But it's me he's staring at, not her. He moves closer, *boing, boing, boing.*

'Never seen that one before,' remarks Summer, admiringly. 'He's a handsome fella!'

I look at his big soft eyes.

I look at his beautiful long eyelashes.

I look at the distinctive white E on his chest.

'It's Eric!' I shout and he does a little sideways hop, skip and jump, and leaps joyfully towards me.

Chapter 9

'That big critter follows you guys everywhere,' remarks Aunty Sheila, a few days later. 'Like a faithful dog.'

'Like Jellico,' says Stanley.

We're all sitting on the veranda after breakfast. Eric is lying in the shade of a bush, a few feet away from us.

It's already hot. You know when people say it's baking hot? Well, it really is in Australia. Uncle Bruce proved it by frying an egg on the path for his breakfast.

'Jellico,' repeats Anika, longingly.

We all miss our lovely dog that we had to leave behind with Rupert Rumble. Bandit, Bess and Bluey fill the gap a bit but they spend most of their time working. I miss my rabbit Hiccup too but I know he'll be fine. My friend Lucinda is looking after him for me till I get back.

Eric has kind of taken their place.

'He likes us more than his kangaroo mates,' says V. Eric flicks his ear lazily. He knows that we're talking about him.

'He's one of the family,' says Mum and stretches lazily. 'Mmm, this is the life.'

'He likes Mattie best,' says Summer, and V pulls a face. But it's true and to prove it I stand up and move out to the yard. Immediately Eric gets up and hops after me. Everyone laughs, even V.

I know why he likes me. It's because we're so similar.

These are the things Eric and I have in common:

1. We are both vegetarian. Strictly speaking I'm vegetarian and he's a herbivore, that's what Summer said (she knows everything). That means neither of us eat meat. I had vegemite toasties for breakfast and he had grass and everyone else had bacon and eggs.

2. We've both got brown eyes, but his eyelashes are a bit longer than mine. Quite a lot longer, actually.

3. We've both got distinctive marks. I've got freckles on my face (even more since I came to Australia) and he's got a white E on his chest.

4. We both like hopping, only I hop on one leg and he hops on two.

5. He's a worrier. Like me. I know this because he follows me around all the time, checking up on me.

I bet if Eric could, he'd make lists too. I wonder if you can teach a kangaroo to write? Or talk?

'What shall we do today?' asks Mum.

I don't mind what we do so long as Summer and Jayden are with us.

Luckily they are because they're on holiday from school.

'Nothing,' groans Dad. 'It's too hot.'

'Let's go swimming!' suggests Summer.

'**YEEEES**!' we all shout.

'Dontie's really good at swimming,' remarks Stan.

'Cool!' says Summer. She looks at Dontie and his face does that going-red-thing again.

'So am I!' says V.

'So is Summer,' says Jayden. 'And me!'

'Fancy a race across the dam, Dontatello, little fellow?' asks Summer. Summer is joking, by the way. My brother is way taller than her.

Dontie mumbles something indistinct. I wonder if he's got heat-stroke? He's been acting weird ever since we got here.

'I've got a better idea!' booms Aunty Sheila. 'Let's all go to the coast.'

'YAAAAY!' The kids rush around gathering together stuff for the beach while the grown-ups sort out the bush-tucker (this is an Aussie phrase for picnic, in case you've forgotten). Then we all pile into the mini-bus.

I catch sight of Eric through the window, watching me with big, sad eyes.

'Aunty Sheila? Can Eric come with us?'

Jayden looks at me as though I'm mad.

'You can't take a kangaroo on a bus!'

'Why not?'

'It's like taking a horse or a cow or ... an elephant ... on a bus. You just can't.'

When he puts it like that I can see his point.

'Aw, Mattie love, Eric'll be just fine,' says Aunty Sheila. 'He can stay here and watch the farm for us.'

'All present and correct?' asks Uncle Bruce, jumping into the driving seat.

'Still waiting for Dontie,' says Mum and rolls her eyes.

V pokes her head out of the door. '**DONTIE!!!!**' she yells and my brother emerges from the house.

He's changed his T-shirt and gelled his

hair. Dad winks at Mum and she grins back at him. What's going on?

'Room here for you,' says Summer, budging up.

'It's alright,' mumbles Dontie, slipping into the back beside me even though it's a smaller space.

Pooh! What's that smell, I wonder silently.

'Pooh! What's that smell?' V says aloud and holds her nose. 'It's deodorant! Dontie, why have you put so much deodorant on? It stinks!'

'Enough questions, V,' says Mum firmly and V says, 'It's not fair!' and folds her arms and frowns out of the window.

Dontie's face is on fire.

As we pull away I wave to Eric standing

in the yard and he waves back.

He looks sad. I hope he'll be okay on his own.

I start to write a mental Worry List to think about later.

1. Will Eric be lonely without us?

2. What's wrong with Dontie?

Chapter 10

It's a long way to the coast. We bowl along a bare road, lined with little more than scrub and the odd tin-roofed, one-storey house, raising clouds of red dust behind us. Uncle Bruce teaches us the song about gumtrees, plumtrees, a sheep-or-two-and-a-kangaroo, and an old rocking chair, and we sing it at the tops of our voices, word perfect.

Galahs (pink and grey birds like parrots) rise squawking into the trees.

We hardly see a soul, just the occasional farmer in a ute going the other way. (A ute is a small open truck.) Uncle Bruce sounds his horn and we wave.

It's really fun. Then I remember Eric.

'Will Eric be alright?' I ask Dontie, worriedly. 'He won't try and follow us, will he?'

'No, it's too far.'

'Actually, kangaroos can travel for long distances at up to speeds of 40 miles per hour if they want to,' says Jayden, who collects facts.

'Wow! That's nearly as fast as we're going!' says V.

'Slow down, Norman!' instructs Aunty Sheila (Norman is Uncle Bruce's real name, but that's another story). 'We don't want Hop the Cop after us!'

'Stop fussing, woman!'

'Who's Hop the Cop?' asks Dad.

'Sergeant Hopper, the policeman in charge of this area. Very keen. He wants to be Inspector,' explains Aunty Sheila.

'Hop Cop wants to be Top Cop,' says Lorabelle. 'Mum reckons he gets points for every summons he issues.'

'Kangaroos can leap really high and long, like about 10 metres at a time,' continues Jayden.

Lorabelle's laugh is loud and throaty, like Aunty Sheila's. 'My son, the walking encyclopaedia!'

I must remember to add these interesting facts about kangaroos to my *Interesting Facts About Kangaroos* list.

'What's that noise?' asks V who's got really good hearing.

'What noise?' asks Uncle Bruce and Uncle Vez who are both pretty deaf.

'That high, whiney noise,' says V. 'Listen!'

Everyone goes quiet. I can hear it now. 'It's coming from behind us.'

'It's getting louder,' says Dontie, next to me in the back, and we turn around to take a look. 'I can't see anything, there's too much dust.'

'I can see a flashing light!' shouts Stanley who's got sharp eyes.

'Uh – oh!' says Lorabelle.

'Is it a fire-engine?' asks V.

'Is it an ambulance?' I say, peering through the dust.

'Sounds more like a police car to me,' says Jayden.

'It *is* a police-car,' says Stanley, his face

shining with excitement.

'It's Hop the Cop!' screeches Aunty Sheila. 'Norman! I *told* you to slow down!'

Uh, oh! **Worry Alert!**

'Yay!' shouts V in excitement. 'Car chase!'

Uncle Bruce pulls over to the side of the road and Hop the Cop gets out of his car, pulling his notebook out of his top pocket. He's not very tall, with a long, mournful face.

Anika is excited too. When Mum winds the window down so Hop the Cop can take a look inside, Anika pats him on the top of his head. He looks a bit surprised and turns to Uncle Bruce.

'How you doing, Norm?'

'Good, Hop.'

'You in a hurry?'

'Off to the ocean, Hop. Got some visitors over from England.'

Hop leans in to look at us and Anika plants a kiss gently on the end of his nose. I think she likes him.

I'm not sure anyone else does. Especially when Hop says, 'By rights I should slap a ticket on you, Norm.'

'Sorry Hop. I thought I was well inside the speed limit,' says Uncle Bruce, looking meek and apologetic.

'Not so sure about that, Norm. You see, you just came through a built-up area.'

Anika pats Hop's cheeks and giggles. Hop's solemn face gives way to a smile. He chucks Anika under the chin and tucks his notebook back into his pocket.

Everyone breathes a sigh of relief.

Then Grandma snorts.

'Call this a built-up area?'

'Marjorie ...' warns Lorabelle, but Grandma continues regardless.

'Do you mean that scruffy-looking house we passed with a pile of junk in the garden?'

'Marge, that's enough,' whispers Aunty Sheila urgently, but Grandma takes no notice. When she's on her high horse no one can stop her.

'Sheila, I'm merely pointing out to the nice officer that it doesn't matter if we drive past it a little faster than we should. The place was derelict. Nobody lives there.'

Uncle Bruce, Aunty Sheila and Lorabelle groan.

Hop's smiley face has turned sour. 'Actually, Madam, somebody does.'

'Really?' says Grandma in surprise. 'Who in their right mind would live there?'

Hop pulls his notebook back out. 'Me.'

Chapter 11

Hop the Cop licks the end of his pencil.

'Name?' he asks, with it poised above his notebook.

'You know my name, Hop,' says Uncle Bruce, wearily.

'Just doing my job, Norm,' he says importantly. 'Breaking the speed limit is breaking the law.'

'Bruce,' says V helpfully. 'His name is Uncle Bruce.'

'Bruce?' Hop the Cop writes it down

then looks puzzled. 'I always thought your name was …'

'Eric,' says Anika brightly.

Hop the Cop tears the page out of his book and starts again. 'Eric,' he says, writing it in.

'No, it's not Eric,' I say. 'And it's not Bruce either. Bruce is his nickname, not his real name. Like Uncle Vesuvius.'

'Vesuvius?' says Hop the Cop, ripping out that page too. 'How do you spell that?'

'V-E-S-U-V-I-U-S,' says Stanley who's good at spelling. Hop the Cop copies it into his book carefully, his tongue sticking out between his teeth, just like V when she's concentrating.

'But his real name is Albert Trot,' I explain. 'That's just a nickname.'

'Albert Trot?' Hop the Cop tears a third page out of his notebook and scratches his head. 'I always thought his name was Norman Trot.' He writes **ALBERT TROT** in his notebook in big letters.

'That's not him. It's him.' I point to Uncle Vez.

'How-do?' Uncle Vez raises his hat politely and Hop the Cop does a double-take as he notices for the first time two Uncle Bruces in the car.

'Eric,' repeats Anika.

Poor Hop the Cop. He's getting very confused. It's time for introductions.

'This is Uncle Vesuvius, only he's really Albert Trot, and this is Uncle Bruce, only he's really Norman Trot,' I explain.

'So who's Eric?' says poor Hop, scribbling it all down.

'Eric!' announces Anika for the third time as if that explains it.

Then I notice that she's pointing past the policeman to the side of the road.

Hop the Cop turns around and steps back and at last I can see what Anika could see all the time.

A kangaroo is standing patiently under a tree.

'That's Eric!' I yell. 'He must've followed us after all!'

He bounds over to the car in one huge leap and lands by Hop the Cop who takes a step back in alarm. Eric stands up on his hind legs and looks at him squarely in the eye. Then he does a funny thing.

He puts his front legs up like he wants Hop to play boxing with him.

We all laugh. But I don't think Hop thinks it's funny because, to my surprise, he:

1. yelps

2. backs away

3. makes a mad dash for his car

4. tugs it open

5. dives in

6. starts up the car

7. chucks a u-ey (this is Australian for making a U-turn) and

8. disappears, wheels screaming, back the way he came

'He's speeding!' remarks V. 'That's against the law, that is.'

'He's dropped his notebook,' observes Dontie.

Eric hops over and picks up it up, nibbles it delicately, then wolfs down the whole lot in big bites, chewing and swallowing until it's all gone. After that, he licks his lips, bounds back to the side

of the road and lies down under his tree.

'Thanks mate,' says Uncle Bruce. 'Have a good rest and we'll see you on the way back.'

I wave to Eric and he waves back and we continue on our way to the coast, singing about *a-sheep-or-two-and-a-kangaroo*. Only now *I'm* sitting in the front passenger seat. I've got an important job to do.

I'm keeping watch on Uncle Bruce so he doesn't exceed that pesky speed limit again.

Chapter 12

It's nice to be beside the seaside. Australians call it the ocean. The beach is long and wide with big surf and it's like being in Cornwall on holiday, only ten times hotter. It's so hot you need to wear sunscreen *and* cover up so we Butterfields keep our T-shirts on over our swimsuits. It's lucky we've got our cork hats.

Jayden's got a green and black wetsuit and Summer's got a pink and black one. She looks fab. I wish I *was* Summer.

I think Dontie does too because he can't stop looking at her.

She's got some bright green and yellow florescent sun cream that she spreads in stripes on her face and it's really cool. She lets us use it and she spreads some on baby Will who looks so cute. All the grown-ups say, 'Aaw!' (*Aaw!* is Australian for *Ahh!*).

She tries to dab some on Dontie but he jerks his head away and says, 'Gerroff!' and everyone laughs. Dontie walks away, his face on fire.

Summer looks hurt. She grabs her pink body board and runs off down to the ocean.

I don't know what's wrong with Dontie. He acts like he doesn't like Summer but I think she's really nice.

Stanika, V, Jayden and I leave him

alone and go off exploring the beach. Jayden is good at finding stuff and knows loads. He reminds me of Will. Not my baby brother Will but a boy I met on holiday in Cornwall (there was something very special about *that* Will which I can't tell you about now because it's another story).

We find things we've got at home and things that we've never seen before in our lives.

After a while Dontie turns up, though he doesn't join in. He just sits chucking stones into a nearby rock pool, looking moody.

I don't care. The beach is really interesting.

Here is a list of things we find that I recognize:

1. Limpets, periwinkles and barnacles, clinging to the rocks

2. Crabs, scuttling out of our way

3. A starfish. Jayden says if they lose one of their legs they can regrow another one. I never knew that. That is so useful!

4. Seaweed. Only this seaweed is special because it's called DEAD MAN'S FINGERS!

Here is a list of things we find that I've never seen before:

1. A fish called a blowie. Jayden tells us it's also called a weeping toadfish

or a pufferfish (how can one little fish have 3 such cool names?)

2. A seahorse. I always wanted to see one of these! Well, we think it's a seahorse because it's that sort of shape, but it's dead and a bit crumbly so it's hard to tell. Jayden says it might be a sea dragon which is even more exciting. (It's little though, not big like a real dragon.)

3. A sponge (this is a real living creature, not a cake or something you wash with)

4. A turban snail which is a snail shaped like a turban

5. Best of all, a bobtail lizard, sunbathing in the dunes. It looks like a mini dinosaur. When it sees us it rears up onto its back legs, opens its jaws wide and hisses at us. It's got a blue tongue and looks scary but Jayden says it's harmless

'What's the most dangerous creature in Australia?' asks V.

Jayden thinks for a minute. 'A croc?'

'Are there crocodiles here?' I ask, looking around fearfully. Stanley pulls Anika closer to him.

'Not on this beach,' says Jayden. 'You get the occasional shark swimming in though.'

'Yeah, right,' says Dontie scornfully.

Why is he being like this?

'It's true,' says Jayden. 'There's even been the odd shark attack, though it's pretty rare.'

I look at the blue ocean with its white-fringed waves. People are playing, swimming, surfing in it. It's a fun place to be. Summer's down there somewhere, on her pink body board.

Suddenly, a terrible piercing, shrieking, wailing sound blasts us and I nearly jump out of my skin. Anika leaps into Stanley's arms.

'What's that?' yells V.

'It's the siren!' shouts Jayden, springing to his feet.

It's one of the loudest and scariest noises I've ever heard in my life. Worse even than the plane taking off.

'What's it for?' I clamp my hands to my ears and stare out to sea. Everyone is dashing out of the water.

'Shark alert!' says Jayden.

A rescue boat is tearing across the shore just beyond the surfers. It turns, comes back and does the same thing again but a bit further out.

'Stanika! V! Mattie! Dontie!' Mum and Dad are charging down the beach behind us, closely followed by the others.

'Oh, thank goodness!' says Mum. She grabs Anika from Stan and whisks her up into her arms then hugs us all.

'Jayden? Where's Summer?' asks Lorabelle in a little, uncertain voice.

Dread creeps over me, like an octopus, with cold, clinging tentacles.

'**SUM-MER!!!!!!!**' yells Dontie and sprints off down to the ocean.

Chapter 13

It's all right. Don't worry. All's well that ends well.

That's what they say in books.

We chase after Dontie and when we get to the shoreline V shouts, 'Look!'

That's when we see them. Dontie's hugging Summer and she's smiling up at him and hugging him back.

Summer hasn't been eaten by a shark after all.

Lorabelle grabs Summer and hugs her too.

'Mu-um!' says Summer, wriggling away. 'Stop fussing.'

Mum winks at Dad. 'She never said that to Dontie.'

We stand amongst the crowd on the shoreline watching the boat shooting to and fro.

'What's it doing?' asks Stan.

'Chasing the shark away from the beach,' explains Uncle Bruce.

V elbows me in the ribs. Dontie and Summer are holding hands.

'Is Summer Dontie's girlfriend now?' she whispers.

'I think so,' I whisper back and we giggle.

Dontie glances over. He heard us! But

instead of going red, he grins.

At last the siren stops and everyone cheers and claps as the boat returns to the shore.

'Where's the shark?' asks Anika, from the safety of Mum's arms.

'Gone back to its mummy,' explains Mum.

Suddenly sharks don't seem scary anymore.

'Shall we have a barbie?' asks Uncle Bruce.

'**YEEEEESSSSS!!!!!!**' A barbecue sounds delicious!

We collect driftwood while Aunty Sheila and Grandma unpack the food they've brought with them and Dad and Granddad go off to buy fresh fish. Soon Uncle Vez and Uncle Bruce have got the fire alight between them but they say it's best to leave it for a while until the embers have died down.

We have a dip in the ocean because the shark has gone now, though Mum and Lorabelle keep watch JUST IN CASE! Australian sea is practically *boiling* compared to Cornish sea. Summer is showing Dontie how to surf, though Lorabelle reminds them not to go out too far.

Baby Will sits in the shallows splashing himself, spluttering, blinking and chuckling, in that order, again and again and again.

'He's so cute,' says Summer, watching Dontie falling off the board. 'He's like a little fish. Not like his brother.'

Dontie gets up and flicks water at her

and she splashes him back. They're getting on really well now they're boyfriend and girlfriend.

'Will's a mer-baby,' says Stanley and tells her all about the mermaids we learned about on our last holiday.

Summer says England sounds cool and she'd like to come and visit us there one day. Dontie looks really happy.

'He's not going to need a bath tonight, that's for sure,' says Mum, hauling him out of the water and wrapping him in a towel (Will, I mean, not Dontie). Will kicks and screams in protest. He wants to be back in the nice warm water.

Further up the beach Uncle Bruce and Uncle Vesuvius are stringing fish across the fire. We're allowed to have cheesy corn snacks called cheezils and twisties

while we're waiting for our burgers because **WE'RE STARVING!**

Dontie and Summer are sharing a beach towel.

'You know how we call Stanley and Anika 'Stanika' because they are always together?' says V, crunching away. 'Well, now Dontie and Summer are together too, so I think we should call them Dummer!'

Everyone laughs as Dontie chases V and dunks her in the ocean.

'*I* think, we should call Uncle Bruce and Uncle Vesuvius Uncle Bruvius because they're so alike,' suggests Stanley.

'Good idea!' Aunty Sheila shrieks with laughter and snaps her fingers. 'Bruvius? When's that barbie going to be ready?'

Fish, fresh from the sea, cooked over an open fire, smells delicious. It's hard being a true veggie but I stick to my guns and have a veggie kebab instead (actually, I have six!).

For afters we have fairy bread which is hundreds and thousands on white bread and it's yummy. It must be an Australian delicacy like cheezils and twisties because I've never heard of it.

All of a sudden it gets dark, like the sun has dropped out of the sky. By the time we've finished eating, the moon is up. I lie down on the soft sand, full as a goog (that's what you say in Australia when you're full up) and study the stars. Squillions of them twinkle down at me from the black, velvety sky.

I LOVE AUSTRALIA.

Chapter 14

One day Uncle Bruce drives the grown-ups to the city for a day out. Mum wants to go shopping and get her hair and nails done, Dad and Grandma are doing a tour of museums and art galleries, and Granddad and Uncle Bruvius are going to watch an Aussie Rules football match.

We stay and play on the farm. Aunty Sheila and Lorabelle are looking after baby Will and doing chores in the farmhouse. Summer and Dontie are supposed to be keeping an eye on the rest of us, but it's obvious they'd rather hang out together.

'Fancy a walk?' says Dontie carelessly to Summer. 'You could show me the wild flowers?'

This is my brother Dontie who at home:

1. never walks anywhere if he can help it

2. would never miss a football match

3. has never noticed a flower in his life

Summer shrugs her shoulders as if she's not bothered. 'If you want,' she says, then the pair of them scoot off as fast as they can before anyone else says they want to come with them.

We don't mind. Jayden, V, Stanika, Eric and me, we're a gang. We can do what we like.

We have the best day ever.

'Let's go and set up camp,' says Jayden who seems to be our leader (he is the oldest), and he finds some old tarpaulin in the shed. We spread it over tree stumps in the bottom paddock so we can sit under it when the sun gets really hot.

'What shall we do now?' says V when camp is all set up.

Jayden comes up with the best answer. 'Let's have koonac races.'

'What are koonacs?' asks Stanley.

'I'll show you,' says Jayden and he takes us to a dried-up swamp to find some.

'I can't see any,' says V, disappointed.

'They're buried underground. You have to dig them out,' he says, and shows us how to do it.

Koonacs turn out to be freshwater crayfish like the yabbies in the dam, only bigger. They look like small lobsters.

We pick one each. V chooses first, the one with the biggest claws. Then everyone else chooses till there's just the smallest one left for Eric.

'Now you've got to name them,' says Jayden.

'Let's call them after our best friends,' I suggest. So we do.

These are the names of our koonacs.

Jayden's: Wade

Mine: Lucinda

V's: Lily Pickles

Stanley's: Rupert Rumble

Anika's: Stanley

Eric's: Mattie

This is a good idea on my part. My best friend Lucinda is good at everything. She's bound to win.

We mark out start and finish points on a slope, then line the koonacs up.

'On your marks, get set, **GO!**' announces Jayden and the race begins.

We cheer on our koonacs at the tops of our voices as Jayden picks up a stick and uses it as a microphone, pretending to be a sports commentator.

'Rupert Rumble gets off to a flying start and Wade is following, close on his heels, with Lucinda chasing after

them. And she's not going
to let them get away. Stanley
is coming up slowly on the
outside while, oh dear! Lily
Pickles has turned around and
gone the wrong way! Mattie
appears to have gone to sleep
on the start line ...'

I shout and shout for Lucinda. I shout for Mattie too because Eric can't, but she stays fast asleep.

Then Eric comes over and nudges her with his nose and suddenly titchy Mattie wakes up and starts chasing after the others.

'That's not fair!' yells V whose koonac is speedily making her way back to the swamp instead of the finish line.

'And, oh no! Rupert Rumble
has veered off to the left and
now Lucinda is closing rapidly
on Wade and Stanley's still in
the race. But wait! Here comes
Mattie from the back and, oh,

*my word! She's overtaking
Stanley and now she's caught
up with Wade. Can she beat
Lucinda?'*

No, Jayden doesn't understand. No one
beats Lucinda. Lucinda is top of the class.
She's always a winner.

His voice is trembling with excitement.

*'And here she comes and I've
never seen anything like it.
Mattie and Lucinda are neck
and neck – and there's nothing
in it – and who's it going to
be? They're coming up to the
finish line – and it's MATTIE!
MATTIE is surging ahead!
She's done it! MATTIE is our*

*winner! What an exciting finish
to the koonac races! Well done
Mattie!'*

Disappointment floods through me as my koonac loses but I give Eric a thumbs up to show I'm not a bad sport.

Then suddenly it hits me.

Mattie has beaten Lucinda for the first time in her life.

And even though it's koonacs, not real people, the disappointment drains away and I'm bursting with happiness.

Chapter 15

We put the koonacs back safely where we found them and go in search of lunch. Aunty Sheila is making huge doorstep cheese and pickle sandwiches and long glasses of home-made iced lemonade. Eric peers in longingly as she puts them on the kitchen table.

'Please can Eric come in for a sandwich?' I ask.

'Nope, I'm not having a kangaroo sitting at my table,' says Aunty Sheila.

'Next thing you know, every pesky critter for miles around will be in here, wanting a free lunch.'

I giggle at the thought of kangaroos and sheep and galahs and bob-tail lizards sitting round the kitchen table, helping themselves to cheese and pickle sandwiches. Aunty Sheila gives me a warning look. 'And don't you go saving one for Eric, Mattie Butterfield, it'll give him lumpy jaw.'

'What's lumpy jaw?' asks Stanley, who likes collecting words.

'Gum disease. Where's Summer and Dontie?'

'Gone to look at the wildflowers,' says V.

'Have they now?' says Lorabelle, bringing out a huge tray of chips. 'Well run and tell them lunch is ready. It's too hot to be outside at this time of day.'

Lorabelle is right. The sun is beating down on us and it's so bright it looks like the whole world is shimmering.

We find Summer and Dontie lazing in the branches of a huge tree. We can see Summer's bright blue t-shirt through the leaves. They don't hear us creeping up on them until we shout:

'DONTIE AND SUMMER,
SITTING IN THE TREE,
K-I-S-S-I-N-G!'

'Kids!' says Dontie in disgust, dropping to the ground. But Summer thinks it's funny.

'You know what?' says Aunty Sheila

over lunch. 'I could do with some more emu oil. D'you guys want to come out to the emu farm with me this afternoon?'

'You should go,' says Summer. 'Emus are hilarious.'

So after lunch Jayden, Stanley, Anika and V squeeze into the back of Aunty Sheila's car while I get the front passenger seat because we flip a coin and I win.

'That's not fair!' says V, but it is.

Lorabelle stays at home to put Baby Will down for a nap and Summer and Dontie stay at home too because she wants to show Dontie her history project on the first settlers in Australia.

'I never knew Dontie was so interested in history,' I remark to Aunty Sheila as we drive along. 'He's changed loads since we came out here.'

'I think it's known as growing-up,' says Aunty Sheila and winks at me as though she's said something funny.

It's not too far to the emu farm. The emus are running around outside in fenced enclosures. They look like ostriches with big feathery bodies and skinny legs, and they've got long, bendy necks and little heads.

One of them snatches Aunty Sheila's hanky and runs off with it in its beak.

It can run really fast. Then another emu snatches the hanky off *him* (or her) and then *another* emu snatches it off *her* (or him) and so it goes on.

'They're playing Emu Rules football,' grins Jayden.

'No, they're not, they're playing beakball,' corrects Stanley and he's right because that's just what they are doing.

We look at some baby emus in a big shed and they're really cute, then some half-grown ones which are really gawky, then some emu eggs which are big and beautiful and green.

Aunty Sheila buys some emu oil because it's good for the complexion and the lady in the shop gives her a free hanky.

It's been a great day even though V makes a fuss because Stanley wins the coin toss on the way home and she wants to sit in the front seat. Stanley lets her. Mum would be cross with V if she knew.

I like emus almost as much as I like kangaroos. But they are naughty.

I think if we were animals Stanley would be a kangaroo and V would be an emu.

Chapter 16

I'm sure that time goes faster Down Under. There's so much to see and so much to do and everything's spread out and a long way away.

One day we travel in one direction for hours in our bright yellow mini-bus just to see a statue of a ram.

The next day we travel in the other direction for hours to see a rock which is shaped like a wave.

Dontie sits in the back with Summer

now, not me. They hold hands and whisper to each other.

'Bor-ing!' says V, rolling her eyes but it's true. They're not that much fun anymore.

Never mind. Jayden and Uncle Bruce teach the rest of us more songs while Eric bounces along behind us.

When we drive past his house, Hop the Cop can be seen outside, sweeping and clearing, mending and fixing. 'Much better,' says Grandma approvingly.

'Keeps him off the streets,' says Uncle Bruce and puts his foot down on the pedal. 'Well done, Marge.'

'You know guys, you're running out of time,' remarks Aunty Sheila. 'If there's something else you want to do before you go home, you'd better say now.'

Everyone goes quiet.

I've been trying not to think about going home. I'm not sure I'm ready to leave Australia yet.

I don't think anyone else is either.

Especially Dontie.

And – **WORRY ALERT!** – what am I going to do about Eric when I go home? I can't take him with me. They'd never allow him on the plane.

All of a sudden it feels like the sun's gone in, even though it's still scorching outside.

'Any ideas?' prompts Aunty Sheila gently. I think she's just realized she's put a dampener on the day.

'We could have a return cricket match!' suggests Granddad who won the game for us when we played against Australia at home. But nobody can be bothered, not even Dontie.

Then Jayden brightens up. 'I know! Let's go spotlighting!'

'What's spotlighting?'

'It's brilliant! We go out in the dark on the back of Dad's ute to look for animals that only come out at night.'

'They're called nocturnal,' says Stanley who likes words.

'How can you see them in the dark?' I ask, puzzled.

'We take spotlights with us.'

'Good idea!' says Summer, cheering up too. 'It's ages since we've been. When we get home we'll ask Dad if he'll take us.'

And so, the next night, our very last night in Australia, after a day spent packing, buying last minute presents and saying goodbye to our favourite places on the farm, we all go spotlighting.

Chapter 17

We pile into the back of Mitch's ute at bedtime with a load of torches and drive out into the bush until we're miles away from anywhere. Finally we stop. The trees meet overhead and block out the moon and stars. It's pitch black, silent and *very* creepy.

Only after a while I realise it's not really silent at all. I can hear little soft sounds, creaking and cracking, shuffling and scurrying. Then I see two little beams of light on the ground and grab hold of Jayden who's standing next to me.

'What's that?'

'Switch your torch on and take a look.'

I do as he says and gasp. What looks like a cross between a giant mouse and a miniature kangaroo is staring up at me. His eyes are shining in the dark.

'What is it?'

'It's a woylie. Look, there's another one over there. And another.'

The woylies are scraping at the earth with their sharp claws.

'What are they doing?'

'Looking for food.'

'What do they eat?'

Jayden shrugs. 'Plant stuff.'

'They're vegetarian, like you Mattie!' says Stan.

'You're a woylie!' laughs V.

'No she's not,' says Summer. 'Woylies eat bulbs and roots and fungus.'

'*Fungus?*' V shudders. 'Yuk! I'm glad *I'm* not a woylie.'

But I think they're cute, especially when they sit up and nibble at bits of food, using their front feet like hands.

Uncle Bruce sweeps his torch downwards and upwards, this way and that, then focuses it on a tree. 'Look up, everyone!'

'What is it?'

'A possum.'

'Wow!'

I can make it out clearly on the branch, its long thick tail dangling down. It studies us calmly with big round eyes like baby Will's. Baby Will stares back at it.

It doesn't mind us being here at all.

'A possum is a marsupial,' Jayden informs us. 'Lots of Australian creatures are.'

'What's a marsupial?' asks Stanley who loves collecting new words.

'It means they've got a pouch,' explains Summer.

'I knew that!' says V, but she didn't.

Spotlighting is brilliant. We see loads

of creatures in that dark wood, some I recognise like owls and wallabies and bats and some I've never seen before in my life like quokkas and quolls.

We see a kangaroo too, but guess what? It's Eric. He's followed us. Then, behind him, I spot some more. Eric spots them too and bounces over to make friends.

Then, just as Aunty Sheila says it's time to call it a day, the best thing happens!

I spot a bilby!

Chapter 18

The bilby pops out of a hole in the ground. I recognize it straightaway because Aunty Sheila showed us a picture once when she came over to see us. That's when I told her I wanted to come to Australia to see one for myself.

It's like a cross between a mouse and a rabbit, with a mouse tail and rabbit ears. It's got a long nose and it's the most comical-looking creature I've ever seen in my life.

It runs around, digging and scratching, and then, when it finds a spider, it flicks out a long tongue and gulps it down. We all laugh because it's really funny – though it's not funny for the spider.

'All part of the food chain,' explains Mum, which means it's all right to eat a spider if you're a bilby.

Anika wants to take it home with her but Dad says we can't because it hasn't got a passport.

On the way back to the farm, Grandma sighs with satisfaction. 'Well, I have to say, this trip has been an education for us all.'

'What's been the best bit?' asks Aunty Sheila.

'All of it,' says Grandma but Aunty Sheila says, 'No, you've got to choose.'

'Aussie Rules footie!' say Uncle Vez and Granddad.

'Aboriginal art!' says Dad. 'And finding out about aboriginal culture.'

'Barbies!' says V. 'And singing songs in the mini-bus.'

'Shark alert!' says Stanley.

'Shark alert!' echoes Anika.

'Shopping!' says Mum.

'What about you, Dontie?' asks Aunty Sheila.

'Summer!' Dad says, and everyone laughs.

'And you, Mattie? What have you liked best about Australia?' continues Aunty Sheila.

I consider the question carefully and V groans.

'She's going to make a list.'

'No I'm not,' I say, undecided. 'But I've got two very best things and I can't decide between them.'

'Go on then,' says V generously. 'You can have them both.'

'One is Eric,' I say, looking through the window to see him bounding along as usual. To my surprise, another kangaroo is skipping along beside him. 'Who's that?'

'Looks to me like Eric's got himself a girlfriend,' says Granddad, peering through the window. 'What are you going to call her, Mattie?'

'Um ...' I think for a second. 'Beryl.'

'Good choice,' says Aunty Sheila. 'She looks like a Beryl. So what's your second very best thing, Mattie love?'

'Spotlighting,' I say. 'I can't wait to tell

Lucinda that I've actually seen a real, live bilby.'

'Well, you won't have long to wait,' says Granddad. 'We're off home tomorrow.'

Chapter 19

I rub my eyes.

It's dark inside the plane except for the light from Dontie's screen.

He's watching a movie. Only he's not really. Half the time he's staring blankly out of the window at the black space beyond.

Poor Dontie. It's not hard to work out what he's thinking about. *Who* he's thinking about.

Summer.

We've had our dinner and now they've switched the lights off and most people are fast asleep.

I was too but Grandma got up to go to the toilet and disturbed me. She's back now and snoring loudly.

It's nice zooming home through the night sky. I'm used to the dark after spotlighting. I'm used to flying too.

It's already tomorrow morning in Australia. They're ahead of us.

Bandit, Bess and Bluey will be waking everyone up with their barking.

Lorabelle will be feeding the chooks.

Aunty Sheila will be cooking breakfast.

I wonder if they're missing us.

Probably not. It's a busy day today.

Mitch is going to fix the fence in the top paddock to stop the kangaroos getting in.

Summer and Jayden are going back to school after the Easter holidays.

I wonder what Eric's doing now.

Last night, when we got home from spotlighting, Lorabelle made us damper with maple syrup and Milo, just like she did on our first night. Then we all went to bed.

V went straight to sleep but Summer and I chatted for a while. Then she fell asleep too.

I didn't. I had something I had to do first.

When I was sure the house was silent I got up, tiptoed downstairs and let myself out of the back door.

I had to say goodbye to Eric properly. I didn't want him wondering where I'd gone or why I'd left him.

I could see him in the moonlight, Beryl by his side. I walked across the back yard and leant against a tree next to them.

'I've got to go home tomorrow, Eric,' I said. 'Back to England.'

Eric's ear twitched and he blinked up at me with his soft, brown eyes.

'Don't worry,' I said. 'You've got Beryl now.'

I stood there for a while then I went back inside the house. At the door I turned to look at him. He was curled up next to Beryl, sleeping soundly.

In the morning they'd gone.

Eric will be fine, I know he will.

I'm not so sure about Dontie though. He's going to miss Summer so much. They promised to Skype and email and stuff, but it's not the same, is it?

Suddenly I remember. I reach inside my back pocket and pull out a letter.

The letter in the pink envelope with *Dontie* on the front in Summer's best bubble writing. I promised her last night I would give it to him on the plane.

It's crumpled now. I straighten it out and dig my brother in the ribs.

'What?' he says grumpily.

I hand it to him and his eyes open wide. He tears it open and reads it greedily. Then he turns to me.

'Mattie! Guess what?' His face is alight with excitement. 'Summer's coming over! She's coming to see us next year! And the others!' he adds hastily.

I sit back with a big sigh of satisfaction. We'll see them all again one day. That's good.

I yawn so widely my eyes close and I nearly swallow myself. My eyes close and the plane throbs on through the darkness.

I can't wait to see Jellico, Hiccup, Lucinda, Lily Pickles, Rupert Rumble and all our friends.

I've got so much to tell them about our Aussie adventures.

Won't be long now.

My funny family are going home.

Praise for My Funny Family

'My Funny Family books are so amazing that I've finished them two times! They are funny and they are my favourite books.' – Inayah, age 7

'I want to read them all over again. My favourite character is V because she is a lot like me.' – Erin, age 7

'I am absolutely bowled over at the enthusiasm you have given Daisy to pick up a book and read. She doesn't stop talking about the characters, what they do, what they say, who they are . . . You have changed Daisy's fear of books and the moving words to almost an addiction.' – Sharon, mother to Daisy, age 9

'Hilarious' – *The Guardian*

'Mollie is able to read the My Funny Family books alone but I insist on having them for bed time stories as I do not want to miss out.' – Jo, mother to Molly, age 6

'I have got all the Funny Family books and they are absolutely fantastic. My favourite is Mattie because she is a worrier like me and I keep a worry list. I feel like I can relate to her and what she worries about.' – Beth, age 9

'Sweet and surprising . . . fresh and funny.' – *Books for Keeps*

'Thank you for giving us all the happy hours of reading.' – Mary, Maddy and Molly age 9

'I love all the funny family books . . . you are my favourite author. I have dressed up as Mattie for world book day here in Bournemouth.' Lilly, age 7

'Endearing . . . a fun, funny slice of family life' – *Junior*

Mattie is nine years old and she worries about everything, which isn't surprising. Because when you have a family as big and crazy as hers, there's always something to worry about! Will the seeds she's planted in the garden with her brothers and sisters grow into fruit and veg like everyone promised? Why does it seem as if Grandma doesn't like them sometimes? And what's wrong with Mum?

Read the first book in the hilarious and heart-warming young series about the chaotic life of the Butterfield family.

www.chrishigginsthatsme.com

my **Funny Family**

It's the summer holiday
and the Butterfield family
is going away to Cornwall.
As usual, Mattie has
plenty to worry about.
What if she loses the
luggage she's been put in
charge of? What if someone
falls over a cliff? And
worst of all ... what if
they've forgotten someone?

Read the second book in the hilarious and
heart-warming *My Funny Family* series.

www.chrishigginsthatsme.com

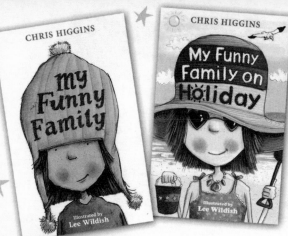

Collect all of the
My Funny Family
books and
discover more
of Mattie's
adventures